The Teens can choose prison for life ... or they can go on a game show called The Caves.

If the Teens beat the robot monsters, they go free.
If they lose, they die.

I am Zak. Sometimes I help the Teens.
Sometimes I don't.

The Teens were called Ellie and Mark. They looked angry. They ran to the caves.

The Voice spoke.

"The game begins in 10 minutes."

THE
CAVES

SNAKE

ENJAMIN HULME-CROSS

Illustrated by
Nelson Evergreen

A & C BLACK
AN IMPRINT OF BLOOMSBURY

First published 2014 by A & C Black,
an imprint of Bloomsbury Publishing Plc
50 Bedford Square
London WC1B 3DP
Bloomsbury is a registered trademark of Bloomsbury Publishing Plc

www.bloomsbury.com

ISBN 978-1-4729-0102-6

A CIP catalogue for this book is available from the British Library.

Printed and bound in India by Replika Press Pvt Ltd

1 3 5 7 9 10 8 6 4 2

I went after the Teens into the big cave.

Ellie was angry with Mark.

"This is all your fault!" she said. "You should be here on your own."

Mark laughed at Ellie.

I did not want to help this boy but I took two axes
out of my bag and put them on the ground.

Then I went back outside.

There was a cage on the rocks. The cage door
opened. A huge snake crawled out.

I went back into the caves.

The Teens had picked up the axes.

"It's a snake," I told them.

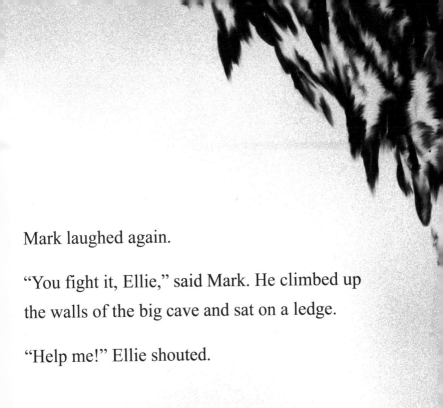

Mark laughed again.

"You fight it, Ellie," said Mark. He climbed up the walls of the big cave and sat on a ledge.

"Help me!" Ellie shouted.

Ellie ran to one of the tunnels. I ran with her.

We both crept along the tunnels.

At last we got back to the big cave.

But now we were high up. Higher than Mark.

The snake crawled into the cave. It looked around for the Teens.

Ellie threw a rock at Mark.

Mark fell off the ledge. He fell to the ground.

The snake looped around Mark.

He tried to stand up but the snake trapped his legs.

He tried to hit the snake with the axe, but the snake trapped his arms.

The snake's jaws opened wide.

Mark screamed.

"Hurry!" I said to Ellie.

Ellie climbed down to the ground.

She swung the axe. She hit the snake's neck.
The snake dropped Mark.

Ellie swung the axe again. She chopped the
snake's head off.

"Mark?" said Ellie.

Mark did not move. Ellie began to cry.

The Voice said.

"Game over!"

Read more of

THE CAVES

SERIES

DOGS

DRONE

LION

LIZARD

SNAKE

SPIDER